DIE

Nigga

DIE

VOLUME 1:
A BLACK MAN'S COMMENTARY

Glen D. Brady

DIE Nigga DIE
Copyright © 2022 by Glen D. Brady

ISBN
978-1-957895-13-0 (Paperback)
978-1-957895-12-3 (eBook)

My Village

To the highest God; creator of all heaven and earth,
and everything within

To the motherland of Africa; the birthplace
of all civilization

To the Beauty, the Knowledge and the Love;
of my beautiful black brothers and sisters,
"Black is Beautiful."

To a scatter people; whose identities were stolen
and replaced with the spirit of a"nigga."

To my wife Pamela, my children, grandchildren, and my
dear decrease mother-in-law Rozzie Coley, our beloved
families combine and extended family, thank you

To my dear decrease mom Verda Mae Brady; and my aunts: Vetra,
Rudy, Vera, Daisy, Molly and Rose and my uncles: Lee, James and
Lonnie(Nola) who raise my cousins and me as a village, thank you

To the man I call dad; James Henry who took on the responsibility of
five kids; plus one, and made us a family with my mom, thank you

To my spiritual mother, Mattie L. Taylor and my
spiritual father Reginald R. McGill thank you

This book is dedicated to what you believe you are, not
what they say you are, "no niggas here, just family."

CONTENTS

STATEMENT

THE MOST LIKELY lie that the black man or the black women have undertaken is the word "Nigga", as an expression of endearment. The nigga spirit was indoctrinated into our Black African ancestors as slaves, here in the United States of America, by white American slave owners and other whites. Do you think that our Black African ancestors in the Continent of Africa, went around calling each other nigga, saying; "what's up my nigga," when they greeted one another? We know that a lie can resemble truth if one continued to accept it as the truth.

Urban Dictionary / Nigger

NIGGER

A word that in old English is derived from a Latin term meaning ignorant, foolish, uneducated, that has very little to do with race or origin but has been deemed a term for African Americans due to the lack of education they received in the 1800's and early to mid-1900's before the Civil Rights Movement. In current times most African Americans have more access and more funding for education than any other race on the planet but still choose to retain their cultural diversity, therefore still deserving and retaining the term "nigger" which still means ignorant. Less the degree of obscenity and volume used by these people on a regular basis, they are still people and this word is but yet a word and does not need to be displayed toward any particular race but needs to be returned to its original status and not taboo. A nigger is an ignorant cocksucker that is loud and uneducated, without bounds, and worthless to society.

POEM

In my dream, I hear a chant
Expressing the words, "Die nigga die."
It sounded like fans of a football team chanting.
But "Die nigga die," was the chant of these fans
On the playing field, in the middle of the stadium, I see a tree looking
weather-beaten, over time

Its limbs looked stout, and without a doubt, I said to myself, this must
be the hangmen tree; the fruits of this tree are no longer a strange
occurrence, but a regular Sunday event, referring to the chant; "Die
nigga die."

They led me out onto the playing field, a field that many black
professional athletes have lived out their dreams on, and now the playing
fields have become, a political killing field, for the black man and the
black athlete.

Fans waving the American flag, and doing the human wave in their
stadium seats, a chant of "Die nigga die" fills the air, along with the
smell of popcorn and hot dogs

Suddenly I awake to frighten to move, shouting; you want to kill me,
you want to kill me, I want to kill those stereotypes that you have
indoctrinated in me, and I began to chant "Die nigga die" for a different
reason

The nigga spirit has to die! With a quick of burst of"; Black pride", I
shouted;" I am a Black man; of African descent, I'm no nigga", and I
went for a walk in my hood, not as a "Nigga" but as a Black man of
African descent

Don't; "what up my nigga" me, address me as a brother, a fellow Black
man, of African descent.

QUOTATIONS

"Anything that is taught as a method can become a doctrine, and it can be learned and adapted to one's spirit"

-Glen D. Brady

"Can you imagine a child asking a parent "am I a nigger" And the parent respond by saying "yeah but you're the one with an (a) not (er). "How intelligent is that?"

-Cornell Dews

"Niggers was the one on the rope, hang off the thing, Niggas is the one with gold ropes, hang out at the clubs"

-Tupac Shakur

"Yo' so many black men out here trying to be niggas
Keeping it real to the point that they dying to be niggas
When in actuality the fact is you ain't-a nigga because you black
You a nigger cause of how you act
But, you don't want me to tell you the trut, so I'mma lie to you
MAke it sound fly to you"

-Cee-Lo

"When I enter a room occupied by white America, and they are looking at me, like I am something strange (a nigga). The only nigga I see in the room is you, (white America) and your ignorance, your unwillingness to change your views, on those who do not look like you".

-Glen D Brady

INTRODUCTION

LET THE TRUTH be known; I am neither a historian nor a Professor of Black African study, I'm merely a storyteller of factual and fictional events through creative writing. These short stories, poems, rap and song lyrics, and light humor stories in this book are my commentaries of the black man struggles, the black man pride, and the black man frustrations with white America. My wish is that our young black minds and our elders will read these short stories,, poems, rap and song lyrics, and light humor stories in this book and get a vivid picture, of what we wrestle with personally, and collectively, regarding our Black Heritage. The words "Die Nigga Die" is used to depict the stereotypes and the offensive history of its usage in White America and Black America. The word "Nigga" in my opinion is the Greek myths (the Pandora's Box) that let out many evils and ills into the world regarding racism, toward the black man. Enchain him physically, and mentally, never embracing him, and indoctrinated in him a low self-esteem through inhuman treatment (cruelty). History reveals those who pander and sold black African slaves, branded and indoctrinated them into this "nigga spirit" of animalism. Chattel; a piece of property, being unintelligent, unable to live without someone or some corporation to rule over them, telling them what to say, do, wear and think. Even today's mass media panders to these same stereotypes of the black man, and we (black people) go about using these same pandering notions (stereotypes) among ourselves in our community. Thinking that the word nigger or nigga is a word of endearment, we even got other races using the word nigga, as if it is the hippest thing to say in the hood. I believe that a lie is long-lived until it is addressed with the truth. The infamous Willie Lynch wrote a letter some Three hundred years ago, regarding how to control black slaves (the black man). Some will try try and tell you that this letter is a hoax, a myth. Nevertheless, I encourage every black person to seek this letter out for you and find the similarities in today's black culture. In how we as blacks deal with each other, according to the Willie Lynch method, and how we are refueling this method, throughout family generations unknowingly, "Die Nigga Die" (the spirit of a nigga has to die).

Our Black African ancestors did not call themselves niggas in the continent of Africa; this was initiated here in North America. Branded as unintelligent, chattel for a masses workforce, and we (black people) continue with this nonsense, calling each other nigga like it is a badge of honor. Your are dishonoring yourself, and your black ancestors, who walked with their heads held high, with black pride. The usage of the word" Nigga has to die; I say "Die Nigga Die" get the smoke out your eyes, the slang out your talk, stop being mesmerized by the mass media, especial the music industry (hip-hop), stop believing the lie. You are a black man, a black woman, the black family of African descent, with excellent, distinctive contributions to the world, Black History is the world history, white America, and Europeans hide this fact, about black people. In the hearts and minds of both white and black America, the usage of the word "Nigga" has to die. My motto is "No niggas here, just family". I hope you will adopt this same mindset in your community, and that these short stories, poems, rap and song lyrics, and light humor stories will enlighten your hearts and minds to be conscious of the thought; that you're no "Nigga," you're family, the black family of civilization.

EACH ONE TEACH ONE

Written by Glen D. Brady

THREE LITTLE BOYS were playing in the playground just hanging out, being little boys, you see.

One was White, one was Asians, and one was Black, just as simple as that, just hanging out, being little boys.

Through the chain link fence, surrounding the playground, they can see three black men standing across the street, no particular thought of who they might be, no signs of threat that they can see.

They were just three little boys hang out, playing in the playground, just being little boys, you see.

Then Someone asks the three little boys a question; they said to the little boys how many niggas do you see, standing across the street.

The three little boys ran to the chain link fence to see what a nigga might be, just being curious boys, eager to see.

There were three black men just standing across the street, talking to each other, in a half circle of three.

The person asks the little White boy, how many niggas do you see?

The little White boy replied; I see three, I see three

The person asked the same question to the Asians boy. The little Asians boy replied excitedly jumping up and down saying; I see three, I see three

The person looks at the Black boy with an intimidating grin, and said how many niggas do you see?
The little black boy lowered his head, nervously looking down at his feet, he slowly raised his head, and he looked as thought someone else, was looking through his eyes, suddenly his hands grasp the chain link fence with a slight force like he was trapped inside.

He hesitated slightly, before he began to speak, feeling a mighty tug from inside his belly, down to the soles of his feet.

The little Black boy said to the person who had asked the question, how many niggas does he see?

The little black boy said; I don't see any niggas that you see, I see three Black men, who look like me.

The little Black boy did not speak from what history had labeled him to be; he spoke from the tugging he felted inside his belly, down to the soles of his feet, his ancestors tugging on his soul, who once sat up under the Baobab tree, teaching our Black genealogy to the children (the black family).

We must promise to instill the teaching of, the Afrocentric Black man and not the American Nigga in our children's hearts.

I AM NO NIGGA

Written by: Glen D. Brady

Verse: Yo' check this, if you see 3 to 4 black men together, America call it a gang,

If you see 3 to 4 white men together, they say it's not the same.

Verse: You Stop me, frisk me, asking my name, detain me, degrade me, like it's, a game.

Verse: Got me sitting legs cross, hands behind my head, it's insane where a black man, in the twenty-first century, have to tell you where he's going, and his name.

Verse: America is motionless, Jim Crow era, separate but equal word on the street, stop and frisk, Yo' that shit is weak.

Verse: I'm no nigga, you keep pushing me, you gonna find one.

Hook: I holla, die nigga die, I'm no nigga, you keep pushing me, you gona one x2

Verse: Black man, hands up, the Clan patrolling our streets, looking to picnic (lynch) a brother, a father, a sister, a mother

Verse: America think I am a thug out nigga with a gun, you keep pushing me, you gonna find one, Nat Turner creepin, the Birth of a Nation, not the Clansman, but the Black man.

Verse: No more blind eye, our mind is open bringing unity to the streets, our rights to assemble peacefully, and the freedom of speech, bring the double barrel, the voice of the people, flowing down the streets

Verse: I'm no nigga, you keep pushing me, you gonna find one.

Hook: I holla, die nigga die, I'm no nigga, you keep pushing me, you gonna find one

America portrays the black man as being unintelligent, criminal, and sexually aggressive, toward white America.

Sojourner Truth

Written by: Glen D. Brady

NEWS FLASH; BLACKS are rioting in the streets, America has rioted more than any blacks in history, burnt down Black Wall Street in Tulsa Oklahoma, in Rosewood Florida; black people were gun down in the street, the 16th Street Baptist Church bombing, in Birmingham, Alabama. In 1919 alone there were; 26 white on black race riots during that year, racial terrorism on the black community. Blacks have not rioted to such a degree, in trying to annihilate a whole community.

We knew who was wearing those white hooded sheets; the mayor, the police, the white government; you are just like the double mint gum, two faces in one. You give and take, keeping us under your thumb, it's not a thumbprint, but a footprint on our backs. Dirty water to drink, no books in schools, no jobs on streets, you give us nothing, it's hard to be a black family. When we are, too busy trying to pick the locks, of the shackles, on our feet to survive.

You want us to fight your wars, Black Veterans of wars, fought and died, you called them niggas, stole their patriotism, their pride, refugees you treat better than me. America never did anything for blacks' unless it fitted her needs, what you gave us, we could have got on our own, I do not see any white men in your history book, hanging from no tree, and you call me a nigga, the spirit you indoctrinate me.

Die nigga die, the spirit of a nigga has to die; America is the aggressor, keeping this negative, confrontational image alive about (me) the black man and the black family.

Truth is never hidden; you got to be willing to seek it out, and when you find it, let it lead you to the reality that you seek.

-Glen D. Brady

THE MONEY GOD

Written by: Glen D. Brady

GHETTO FAMOUS, FANCY cars, you cannot serve two masters; both money and God, selling dope, a ghetto superstar, having a slave mentality servant to the money god, shackles on your feet. America sends you out to push poison in her streets, a sellout to the black community killing your own (peeps) people.

Hip-hop soul ties, with America diabolical mind, preaching dope man, dope man to our young black minds. You make it sound easy, whipping them up into a frenzy, tattoo's, gold chains, gold teeth, the shine, youngins losing their mind, bout to go all out, school dropouts. The mass destruction you leave behind; tweakers, starving babies, prostitution, robberies, and black on black crimes, your state of mind is similar to the Clan; lynch the black man. Hip-hop is that nigga that America uses to destroy the black family, you can't serve two masters; both money and God. America is your porcelain pagan god that you bow down to, America hides the fact regarding the truth, took the black man history out of the world history book, the historical document containing the truth about the black man. Hip-hop artists is done with you, and looking for that next ghetto star, to put the gun to his or her head, eager to sell his or her soul, homo sold, to say what he or she is told, to destroy the black family deliberately. The Illuminati (the Money god), smoke and mirrors, mesmerizing the young ghetto mind. The Illuminati Street code is; give a nigga a chance to make some money, and use him or her to destroy other niggas, in the process. Then leave that nigga that they use to destroy other niggas, out in the cold broke. It's not about records (CD's), it's about killing the black soul (the black family).

America diabolical plan is; to use and control, to contain, and destroy the black family, through media contents, using the power of media to corrupt and destroy thousands, even millions of black souls, this is how souls are sold, at the price of a Hip-hop song.

Slavery 2017

Written by; Glen D. Brady

A SLAVE BOY from the eighteen hundred, cross over into the future, the year twenty-seventeen. He seen new black boys with gold chains around their necks and their wrist, he thought to himself, are these the black kings that I have seen in my dreams.

He was amazed that the new black boys had clear backs, no whip marks to be seen. Though his clothes were made out of old rags, torn and tattered, he thought it was funny, to see the new black boys wearing their paints, down off their butt, toward their knees. The slave boy had no shoes on his feet, and he felt no shame, he looked and stared at the brand, on the new black boy's feet, thinking slave master name (Nike, Adidas, Reebok, Jordan).

To his surprise, the new black boys were not working, just hanging in the streets, he heard noises that sounded like slave catches cursing and auctioneers selling. (The hustle and the commotion of the inner city, chants of drug dealers selling, police siren, the sounds of people meeting and greeting each other in the city streets)

The slave boy couldn't believe what he was seeing, and hearing, thinking no slave master, and no overseer to see, niggas doing nothing, are they free?

The slave boy pondered, on all that he had seen and heard, he said to himself; niggas will continue to be slaves, even though they are free, this is a different type of slave mentality when you don't know what to do with yourself, in the twenty-first century.

The Emancipation Proclamation freed us from slave states, but not from the slave mentality of dependency. Do we still need to be told what to do?

GANG IN BLUE

Written by: Glen D. Brady

Hook: Gang in Blue, what you gonna do, good cops are bad cops, they see what the bad cops do, hiding behind their badge, who's snitching on you.

Verse: Serve and protect, black people cringe when you roll by, stop and frisk, homo pat down, I'm going to jail or get shot down, public safety, who's protecting me, from you.

Hook: Gang in Blue, what you gonna do, good cops are bad cops, they see what the bad cops do, hiding behind their badge, who's snitching on you.

Verse: Police brutality, clansman riding in blue, hype up on, gangsta rap, and prescription pills, ready to buck break you.

Verse: Tie me around a tree, buck break me, degrade the black man in front of his family, mother scared for her son, sister crying for her brother, father cringes as he watch in silent, he been in that position before, America is the one who breeds ignorance and violence.

Hook: Gang in Blue, what you gonna do, good cops are bad cops, they see what the bad cops do, hiding behind their badge, who's snitching on you.

Verse: Make America great again, gentrification in the black lands, lock us up to push us out, Donal Trump has a hell of a plan, we have to pray on our feet, and resist the genocide of the black family.

Hook: Gang in Blue, what you gonna do, good cops are bad cops, they see what the bad cops do, hide behind the badge, who's snitching on you.

Over policing our neighborhoods and police, brutality has gotten out of control. Who is policing the police (the gang in blue)?

Laugh Out Loud

Written by: Glen D. Brady

THE BEST WAY to know you is to laugh at yourself, at the things (you) we say and do.

They year Thirty seventeen, niggas will be driving spaceship with 144" inch tires, with spinning rims, 1.2 million watts speakers in the trunk, vibrating stars, and shit. Got a pair of silver bull balls hanging under the backend of the spaceship, holding up space traffic talking to his homeboy, got a three-piece box of Popeye's chicken on the front seat, with a blunt in the ashtray.

The year Thirty seventeen, black girls will still be going to Family dollar stores, in pajama pants, with an " I love pink" t-shirts on, with a black shower cap on their heads, shopping for hair glue and deodorant, looking like they just got out of bed.

The year Thirty seventeen, niggas going to be hanging out in front of space transportation stations, selling bootleg DVD's, two for five, three for ten, socks, and generic cigarettes. Going to the barber shops and hair salons, trying to sell you stuff you don't even need like; bicycle inner tubes, VCR's, a set of dishes, the box says, an eight-piece set, and there are only three plates in the box.

They year Thirty seventeen, young black mommas are still going to be cursing their kids out. Sit you dumb ass down, get your dumb ass in there and put those power hot dogs in that dam microwave, for you and your brother and sister. Don't say shit to me; my show is on, don't mess with that dam Kool-aid, till you are finished eating, and get your damn hand, out your damn nose.

Behaviors can last throughtout a lifetime, and be refueled through generations.

-Glen D. Brady

THE GROCERY PUSHCART PEOPLE IN THE HOOD

Written by: Glen D. Brady

A LITTLE TWO-YEAR -OLD black girl was looking out the window in her home, and she saw a person pushing a grocery cart with a gas grill in it. The little girl turned to her mother and said mommy, mommy, store, store, and the mother replied, no store, no store, and the little girl turned back around and started looking out the window again.

The little girl saw another person pushing a grocery cart with a lounge table and chairs in it. The little girl turned to her mother again and said mommy, mommy, store, store, and the mother replied, no store, no store, and the little girl turned back around and stared looking out the window again.

On turning back around a third time looking out the window, the little girl saw another person pushing a grocery cart with a lawnmower in it. Once again, the little girl turned to her mother and said mommy, mommy, store, store, and the mother said no store, no store, we will go to the store tomorrow.

The little two-year-old black girl said to herself, okay mommy, tomorrow you will find out, that the grocery pushcart people have stolen all our stuff tomorrow, when we go in the garage, to get into the car, to go to the store tomorrow.

Are the grocery pushcart people thieves, or are they just trying to survive? What's on the street curb is free, what's in my yard is not. The People verse the Grocery pushcart people, "A black Hood Crime Story," the jury is still out.

AFFIRMATIVE ACTION

Written by: Glen D. Brady

A BLACK MAN went to a job interview at an all-white company in 1963. The white man said to the black man in a playful manner, if you can answer this riddle, I would give you a job here.

He said many niggers had come here looking for a job, but none could answer the riddle. The black man said okay, if that what is going to take, for me to get a job here, what is the riddle?

The white man said; three niggas were knocking on a door, one went in, one came out, and the other one' no one has seen him as of yet. In a serious manner leaning forward, the white man said again, if you can answer this riddle, I will give you a job here; I am a man of my word.

The black man said okay, I would try to answer the riddle. The black man paused for a few seconds, and the he said okay I think I have the answer, he said a matter of fact I know, I have the answer. The white man said; with a surprised look on his face, what is the answer to the riddle, boy!

The black man said it's simple; the nigga that went in is my present, the nigga that came out is my past, and the nigga that no one has seen as of yet, is my future. The black man concluded the riddle by saying;

sir the answer to this riddle is this; I will always be a nigga to the white man, mo matter what affirmative action sates.

The white man reared back in his chair, astonished by the answer and the black man gave him and said; goddam boy! You are a smart nigger, and you got the job.

We have to create opportunities for ourselves, and economics is power. We are trillions of dollars strong together as black people, the black family.

-Glen D. Brady

A TRIBUTE TO BLACKNESS

Written by; Glen D. Brady

Verse 1: I see a face in the mirror, it seems to be looking back at me, so deep the brown eyes, they say the yes, are the window, of the soul

Verse /Chorus A: Who am I, where did I come from?

Verse2: Can I raise a flag, to show you my pride

Chorus B: Who am I, where am I going?

Verse3: So costly the prize, so many fought for and died

Verse4: I feel like I can reach for tomorrow and build on yesterday, the future of our hope has been paid with many lives, to hold our heads up with pride; this is the flag that I will raise- who am I

Verse/Chorus C: I feel like I can reach tomorrow and build on yesterday, the future of our hope has been paid with many lives, to hold our heads up with pride; this is the flag that I will raise- who am I

Verse / Chorus D: Who am I (X7) As the chorus is being sung; seven children are proclaiming names of black historical leaders; their names and accomplishments' between the chorus cycles of; Who am I. For examples: Who am I; "I am Dr. Martin Luther King Jr; Civil Rights Leader", chorus: Who am I; "I am Thurgood Marshall; the first black Supreme Court Justice…

Verse / Chorus C: I feel like I can reach tomorrow and build on yesterday, the future of our hope has been paid with many lives, to hold our heads up with pride; this is the flag that I will raise ---(who am I (x3))

THE FINAL CHORUS SPOKEN: We are the pride of Blackness

Investing In Ignorance and Economic Demise

Written by: Glen D . Brady

KNOCK, KNOC! SAID (The old Friend nigga)
Who's there? Said (The young nigga)
Nigga. Said (The old friend nigga)
Nigga who? Said (The young nigga)
Me nigga. Said (The old friend nigga)
Me nigga who? Said (The young nigga)

(The old friend nigga) said; you nigga. (The young nigga) said; O' come on in, my old friend, I thought I heard that name before, what can I do for you, my old friend? (The old friend nigga) said; oh nothing, I just thought that I, would drop by, to see how things are going, (the demise of the black community).

(The old friend nigga) said; I like what you'll have done with the community. Asians hair stores, Chinese fast food restaurants, Arab stores, Liquor stores on every corner, Check cashing stores, gangs, drugs, violence. Man in my wildest dream, I could not have imagined regenerating my nigga spirit this far, maybe a few hundred years, but thousands wow!

(The young nigga) said; well we believe in keeping it real, keeping it 100% in the hood. (The old friend nigga) said; are the still using my name nigga? (The young nigga) said; yes, we use it in every rap song. (The old friend nigga) said; how is the family doing (the black family)? (The you nigga) said; momma got six kids and raising four of my sisters kids, and daddy is gone, (The young nigga) said; momma would not let him be the man, daddy said this is contrary to Gods plan. (The old friend nigga) said; nice, very nice, are you working? (The young nigga) said; well yes and no well if you call selling drugs work, well I guess I am working (fo sho).

(The old friend nigga) said, what about the young women, how are they living? (The young nigga) said; they call themselves, bitches, and hoes.

(The old friend nigga) said, what about the fellas, what are they doing? (The young nigga) said; well we wear our pants off our ass, doing dumb shit. We are an investment in privatize prisons, on the Dow Jones; the investors are happy because; prisons that were built to hold thousand inmates are currently housing for thousand inmates. A large percentage of the inmates are of color (black and brown). Then the (the old friend nigga) said; nice, very nice, well my young nigga, I have to go, I will see you in another hundred years or so, and when I knock, just open up the damn door, Nigga!

We as Blacks have to take control of our black community; mentally, spiritually, physically, and economically. For our (old friend nigga); will revisit to see if our community has been swept clean of his spirit, and if not, he will bring with him more diabolical methods to destroy the black community.

THE KELOID SCARS OF WHITE AMERICA SLAVE WHIP

Written by; Glen D. Brady

WHY CAN'T MY mind forget?
My heart, heal?
My body, re-posture?
My spirit, re-live?

Establish institutions of injustice in the United States of America; reminds me of the scars of slavery, "keloid scars" that have not been healed properly, the whipping and torture, the beating and rape, of a free spirit people (black people).

Some (black folks) say; move on from the past, you weren't there, it wasn't you. But we cringe in fear when we hear of an injustice anywhere because we (black people) are still being mistreated everywhere.

We use modern salves to heal our wounds; decent jobs, a four-bedroom home, fancy cars, even being in the same room, with them (whites). I want you to answer this question to yourself; do you think you could have kept it together, after being whipped and tortured, beaten and rape, and made to work the next day, and you could not show any anger or hate? These keloid scars have not healed, to this very day, modern salves cannot heal the pain that we feel. The practice of injustice and discrimination in housing finance, judicial, employment, etc. toward the black man and the black woman, re-open these keloid scars (wounds) every day.

Those of you, who are not of a darker shade of black, you think you are perceived as white, lighter than most, but "One drop" of black blood, is enough to be considered a nigga to most (white America), according to the one-drop rule of racial classification. The audacities of you people (the one droppers') and the prominent Negro's, to say; move on from there. The notion of saying move on from slavery past is an offense to those black slaves who died, because a keloid scar you cannot hide.

America we don't want any apologies because you never apologize, we just want to heal, from the keloid scars that you place on our backs, discriminations, stereotypes, human and civil rights injustices, that have not been corrected. These scars pain us, deep inside.

-Glen D. Brady

AMERICA MOST WANTED; THE BLACK MAN

Written by: Glen D. Brady

I AM RUNNING as fast, as I can, I can barely steady my breath, the road of civil liberties lies ahead, an the hounds of sweltering injustices are on my ass, those same ones that hounded my ancestors in the past. I cannot waste any time looking back, for fear might seize me, and incarcerate me mentally and socially. I have to take my stand let my voice be heard, about the criminalization of the black man. They might catch me, tie me to a tree, and whip me, until I am close to death, like those who ran from slave plantations, who sought to be free, from the cruelty and the animalization of human being, kept in chains (the black man). Today I have become America most wanted" the Black man" because I seek my freedom of speech, my right to assemble peacefully, to protest against America criminalization of the black man without representation, to speak out against white America diabolical plan, to destroy the black man (the black family).

Like those before us, we must take a stand; Medgar Evers, Martin Luther King Jr, James Meredith (Civil Rights). And Malcolm X (Human Rights), Bobby Seal, Huge Newton, Angela Davis (Black Panther Party.) Brothers like; John Huggins and Alprentice "Bunchy" Carter (Black Panther Party). They were leaders in the black community. America put a price on their head, saying; if we can't control them, make them dead. Others they gave a pass, you know whom you are, those hundred thousand dollars, prominent Negro's, sellouts to the white man, talking about helping the black man. The gun scope crosshair of government agencies like; the FBI, CIA and other law enforcement agencies, their shooting silhouette targets are black, like the Black man.

White America, when we use our First Amendment" the freedom of speech," you try to make us out to be, some type of communist party and unpatriotic, because we refuse to be silent. White America criminalization of the Black man is bigger than just saluting a flag, placing one's hand over his or her heart, or Colin Kapernick sitting or kneeling, when the "Star-Spangled Banner" is being played.

One of the lyrics in the "Star-Spangled Banner" says; "the land of the free and the home of the brave." But America excluded the black African man, woman, and child when they brought them over to the colonies, by way of the transatlantic slave trade. No unalienable rights considered, nor liberty, and the pursuit of happiness give to the black Africa slaves. No welcome to America speech given to the black family, just the sole of white America shoe boot up their ass and the crack of her whip on their back.

America uses this song; "The Star-Spangled Banner" as a rallying causes to defend against the British. The thirteen colonies themselves were once considered a communist party, to the crown (King George; the third). America do you remember this protest called; the "Boston Tea Party" in 1773, America sought to be free, from the British government tyrannies. "Taxation without representation is tyranny".

-James Otis

I (the Black man) whether die on my feet. Running as fast as I can, to every city, hamlet, village, and state, telling all my black brothers and sister to rise, stand on your feet, or kneel if they want to in protest, and demand to be heard, as the Black community, (the black family).

"The limits of tyrants are prescribed by the endurance of those whom they oppress."

-Fredric Douglass

The National Anthem of the United States of America, encourage us to utilize our first amendment of speech, to rally against tyrannies. America criminalization of the Blackman without representation is tyrannous. Black people stand up and demand to be heard as the black community.

-Glen D. Brady

AFRICA LOST CARGO

Written by: Glen D Brady

IF THEY, THE Black African slaves could speak from where their captors left their bodies to waste in the sand graves scattered across the Saharan desert; or speak from the Red Sea, the Indian ocean, and the Atlantic Ocean. These oceans floors, canyons, and deep-water trenches are covered with bones of Black African slaves. Slaves that were found dead in the belly of these ships by their captors were thrown over the side of the ships. Slaves were chained to each other, restrained side by side with no room to move; to shit or pee, and they were made eat the little bit of food, that their captors gave them, that barely kept them alive.

Black African men, women and children, who were once free, and proud, were being held captive on these slave ships, living in their stench and filth, like animals fro six to eight weeks. Some slaves committed suicide, when they were brought above on deck for air and stimulation, by jumping off the side of these sips into the murky waters by which their captors traveled, because they refused to be treated like animals.

They would say from their resting place; go your way, go your way my dear brother, my dear sister, my dear mother, my dear father, go your way. Though the journey looks hopeless and fearful, and we cry and murmur in our native tongue; we call on the name of our creator to save us, from such inhuman treatment, as we are forced and beaten, to make this journey across the Saharan, the sea, and the oceans.

Go your way, and remember the old ways, and adapt to the new ways, but hold on to the old ways and our native tongue, so that we may communicate from our resting place. As we lay in darkness in the depth of the sea, across the ocean floors, and scattered across the hard terrain of Saharan, like dunes. Our bodies are deterioration, but our souls are free.

Go your way, and one day we will find our way back to our motherland; across the Saharan, across the sea, and the oceans, where we, were once free. Go your way, my dear brother, my dear sister, my dear mother, my dear father, go your way, and somehow live free.

Approximately 1.2-2.4 million African slaves died during their transport to the New World. I believe it was more than that; you cannot even begin to compare statistics, with any race of people that were treated inhumanely, like the black African people, I am getting a little emotional right now.

If we look at the housing condition in our inner cities, the project housing and building. The mentality of the white America is still; pack them in, in close quarters, side by side, restrain them and give them little to survive on. The statistics of environmental destruction; young black men and women being a production of their environment; drugs, crimes, gang's, single mothers, etc. the casualty rate is extremely high, condition to be a slave to something.

A Young man (Nigga), Conversation

Written by: Glen Brady

TWO YOUNG NIGGAS conversing, in the hood

First Nigga: what up fam, what's good?
Second Nigga: nothing my nigga, what's good with you?
First Nigga: Yo' my nigga this shit is crazy out here, my nigga.
Second Nigga: My nigga, that what's up.
First Nigga: Yo' my nigga you hear that new joint by Jay Z, that shit is official, my nigga.
Second Nigga: My nigga that shit is tight, Jay always bring the heat, my nigga.

First Nigga: My nigga, you heard about that nigga, Dollar bill?
Second Nigga: Yo' my nigga, that nigga be wildlin, my nigga, Dollar got hit with some bricks my nigga, 10 to 15 years, fed time my nigga
First Nigga: My nigga, what about those other niggas, that be with Dollar
Second Nigga: You talking about Bird, that nigga Baby, and that light skin nigga Dirty red, those niggas was with that nigga too. Had all that shit up in that house on Third Street, I heard those niggas were holding it down over there, My nigga, I just got out of three months ago, my nigga, did a straight bid my nigga, no papers nigga

First Nigga: My nigga, where did they have you at, my nigga?

Second Nigga: I was upstate my nigga, at Five Points Correctional Facility my nigga, it's some niggas up there we know

First Nigga: My nigga, ain't shit out here right now my nigga, niggas are snitching, and shit, my nigga, you can't trust a nigga these days, niggas be trying to get the Feds off their ass.

Second Nigga: My nigga, I'm good right now my nigga got a little job right now, my nigga.

First Nigga: My nigga, I got to get this bus, my nigga, to see my P.O,, my nigga, stay up my nigga.

Second Nigga: No shit my nigga, I'm on the Westside with my girl, my nigga

First Nigga: That's what's up my nigga, get with me, my nigga, take my digits, my nigga

Time has changed, but the cycle remains the same. Once the system criminalizes a black man, they done made a nigga, and hopefully not for life, but niggas continue to perpetuate the word nigga, like the definition of it, has changed. It is not a term of endearment for black; it is a derogatory word that rolls off your tongue, just as easy, as the word (nigga) rolling off the tongue of a white person calling, a nigga.

How many of you remember this nursery rhyme:

Eeny, meena, mina, mo,
Catch a nigga by the toe;
If he hollers let him go,
Eeny, Meena ,mina, moe

I song this nursery rhyme when I was a kid, playing tag with my friends back in the 60's not knowing how derogatory this word "nigger" was, and still is, black people just give this some thought, on the usage of the word nigga.

THE GHOST OF AMERICA SLAVERY

Written by: Glen D. Brady

ON A HOT summer night, as darkness being to fade, and the first gleam of day, peek through, and the sound of police sirens have quieted down. And the musical sound of the night hustle in the inner city streets has dropped from a quarter rest, to a half rest musical note, the intermittent slulmber rest, of the inner city streets.

A mother hears her little boy talking in this sleep, saying over and over, where is my shoe, where is my shoe, somebody please help me find my shoe, as she was preparing for work.

That night, in the middle hours of the night, she heard him talking in his sleep again saying; where is my glove, where is my glove, somebody please help me find my glove.

The mother thought her son behavior was quite strange, the things that he was saying in his sleep, but knowing her son, she minimizes her thoughts on what she was hearing and fell back to sleep. At daybreak, as the mother was preparing for her busy work day, she heard her once again talking in his sleep, saying where is my scarf, where is my scarf, can somebody please help me find my scarf.

The mother became frightened, and she did not know what to say or do, she gathers herself together and off to work she went, thinking what should I say, what should I do. As evening approaches, the family is sitting at the kitchen table, and the mother is preparing to serve a pot of chicken stew. She finally said to her son; Johnny why were you saying these things in your sleep; where is my shoe, where is my glove, where is my scarf. And then you would as for help to find these things, with a puzzled look on her face, she said; I was frightened for you, I didn't know what to say or do.

The little boy hesitated and said; mother I haven't lost anything, these are the voices of slaves in my dreams.

The she is the foot of slaves that were cut off by the slave master, and the glove is the hand, of slaves that were cut off by the slave master, the scarf is the broken neck slaves that were hung by the slave master.

The little boy apprehensively said; mother is this not the twenty-first century? What are black folks to do? When the sins of a nation past (slavery) still hunts you.

Slavery is not the sin of a man, but the sins of a nation. Who is trying to sweep it under the rug, telling Black America to move on, to a happier place? My black brothers and my black sisters let us keep the discussion, and the facts of slavery in America face. It is possible that in the next 20 years or so, America will convince our black children that slavery never existed, that we were immigrants looking for work in a new country. The true meaning of the word nigger" an ignorant person", White America has taken it out of the published dictionary.

-Glen D. Brady

SLAVE TRAPPIN VS DRUG TRAPPIN

Written by; Glen D. Brady

FIVE SLAVES RAN away from a plantation in Atlanta, Georgia, at mid-day, they ran into the woods seeking, a path north for freedom. One of the slaves said to the other slaves, we need to find a place to hind until nightfall, and then we will have the cover of darkness on our side, and be able to move around a little more openly. So they all agreed and continued to run through the woods, toward their perception of the north (freedom), looking for a place to hide until nightfall. The runaway slaves came across a patch of woods that was very dense with thick thistles and thorns; they figured that not even the slave catchers would think, that someone would be willing to hide in this thick, dense thistles and thorn patch. Though the slaves knew what the thick thistles and thorns could tear their flesh, they were willing to take that chance. When the five slaves were discovered missing, the slave master, and his son started preparing themselves to go into the woods and search for them. The slave master told his son that a nigga is like an animal or pet; he cannot think for his self, you have to take care of him, just like old duke here, our dog. Then the slave master said to his son; do you remember what you trained, old duke to do. You taught him to fetch and come when you call his name, well son you have to train a nigga the same way. They are naive people, but they know their name, and they will come running, just like old duke here, when you call their name (nigga).

The son said to his father (the slave master), should we take old duke with us? The father sai no, let old duke lay around rest; he had his share of tracking niggas. I told you nigga are simple-minded like animals, we will call, and they will come running just like old duke. So the slave master and his son went off into the woods, searching for the five runaway slaves, in no particular direction.

The slave master and his son, as they walked through the woods, the slave master would shout; is there any niggas here, any niggas here, just walking calmly and shouting; is there any niggas here, any niggas here.

Now the slave master and his son had been walking for a very long time, and the sun seems to be flirting with the late hour of the day.

Walking in no particular direction, they came across a dense, thick patch of thistles, and thorns in the woods. The slave master said to his son, we have been walking for a good while now, those niggas probably done cross over to next country by now, they are like a wild animal, they were probably moving faster than I thought, but we will get them, the won't get far. The slave master said to his son, I'm going to sit here on this rock and rest, it is getting late in the evening, but if you want to give one more shout out (is there any niggas here) you can. Okay the son said; the son begins to shout; is there any niggas here, any niggas here, and all of a sudden they heard a voice coming out of the dense, thick patch of thistles and thorn, saying; no niggas here.

The slave master jumps up off the rock, to his feet with his shotgun in hand, and said you niggas come one out of there, and the slaves came out one by one. The slave master looked at his son with a smile, and said; I told you, son, niggas are simple-minded. Just like old duke, you teach them their name, teach them to fetch and come, and when you call them, they will always respond, and live up to their name, "nigga". God dad boy, you trapped your first niggas, I am so proud of you son.

Slave trappin: slaves train to respond to the name nigga
Drug trappin: the act of dealing or selling illegal drugs

When you place yourself in a dense, thick patch of thistle and thorns, seeking to break away from the oppressor, by dealing or selling illegal drugs, it becomes a hard trap. Psychologically and sociologically you will respond like a nigga, live like a nigga, who has been trained, to think like a nigga. The five slaves that were hiding did not have to say a word, but they responded by how, they were taught to think. They have been living like nigga's, on the plantation, and in their mind. There is nothing positive about the word nigga, in name or deed. Stop living like a white man pet, with a predictable nature. Live like you're proud, to be a black man or a black woman, stop living like a trained animal, trained to do wrong, and trained to be kept down.

Surviving In
Difficult Times

Written by: Glen D. Brady

A BLACK MAN, Mexica man and a White man and his dog, was stranded in a rowboat without paddles. The Blackman said to the other two; well we do not have any paddles to row the boat, so we have to use what God has given us to help get this boat moving.

The Black man asks the Mexican man; what can you use that God has given you, to help us move this boat along, The Mexican man said; I do not know, but I live in a one-room house with fifteen of my relatives, I know how to make use of small spaces. Even to this day, I am the fourth person in a stack of fifteen that I sleep in, (laugh), the Black man said; okay that good.

The Black man asks the White man, what can you use that God has given you, to help us move this boat along. The White man said; well I was the valedictorian of my high school graduating senior class, voted most likely to succeed, and I graduated from Harvard you know, and the Black man said; sure, sure, okay.

The Mexican man said; what about you amigo, what you use that God has given you, to help us move this boat along. The Black man said well; what I can use, that god has given me, is these big ass lips, I can use them as a boat motor, the Mexican man said; that is good amigo.

The Whiteman began to laugh saying, God didn't give you guys much did he. The Black man and the Mexican man looked at each other, and said simultaneously; God gave us enough strength to throw your ass out of this boat. So the Black man and the Mexican man threw the White man out of the b oat. The Mexican man sad to the Black man; amigo what about his dog, the Blackman said: well thedog can use what God has given him. The Mexican man said; what is that amigo, the Black man said; his tail. He can use it as a rudder for the boat, while I motor it with my lips, and you make use of small space and steer the boat to safety. The Mexican man said; awe amigo, I was worried for a moment, for God is good, He will provide, and white entitlement we do not need, senor.

They always thought that they were giving us nothing, if it held no value or taste, give it to the slaves to survive on, but we made something out of their nothing, and today they are still capitalizing on our something, that we made out of their nothing. (think about it)

-Glen D. Brady

THE UNDERGROUND RAILROAD

Written by: Glen D. Brady

THE UNDERGROUND RAILROAD laid its rails across swamps, creek beds and water brooks, they zig zagged through the woods, up and down hills and through valleys, across states lines and country borders. One of the most famous conductors of the Underground Railroad was a short woman. Who had no distinctive features, she wore a bandanna on her head, and her name was Harriet Tubman. Most of the slaves called her Moses; like the Moses of the Bible because she led them to the promised land of freedom. Harried Tubman stated, "I had reasoned this out in my mind, there was one of two things I had a right to, liberty, or death; if I could not have one, I would have the other; for no man should take me alive."

With a lantern in her hand she didn't say much, just nodded and signaled with her hands; to stop, to go or to rest at intervals that she deem to be the best. No tickets were needed to come aboard, no checking of luggage or screening for terrorist. For those who sought freedom, they knew the time, and day when the Underground Railroad was coming their way, and they waited and looked for the signal, to start running toward her way (the Underground Railroad).

As they made their way through the woods picking up passengers from different plantations. The conductor Harriet (Moses) Tubman would say "If you hear dogs, keep going, if you see torches in the woods, keep going, If there's shouting after you, keep going, don't ever stop, keep going, If you want a taste of freedom, keep going."There were many good Quakers and abolitionist along the way; they gave food and shelter to the runaway slaves, the conductor of the Underground Railroad they also knew, they called her Moses too, and pledged to help her make her way, toward the freedom land she knew. Harriet (Moses) Tubman stated, "Quakers almost as good as colored, they call themselves friends and you can trust them every time."

Rounded that last bend, crossing over into freedom land, pulling up to the depot; the home of a Quaker Friend, the passengers were greeted with a smile and were called; friend. They tears and hugged one another; shouts of joy rang out of the mouths, of newly free men and women slaves, thanking God for their deliverance and their deliverer, Harriet (Moses) Tubman.

Harriet (Moses) Tubman stated", I never ran my train off the track, and I never lost a passenger". As the slave's shout of freedom began to quiet down, and tears of joy, continue to stream down the faces of newly freed men and woman. Harriet (Moses) Tubman secretly met with her abolitionist friends, to plan her next trip back to the south, to lead more slaves out of slavery to freedom land.

Harriet (Moses) Tubman stated, "If I could have convinced more slaves that they were slaves, I could have freed thousands more."

If you were to ask the average black fifth grader student, about the Underground Railroad, he or she would probably say; what is that. A subway train that runs underground, taking people around New York City. How in such a short amount of time, black people have forgotten, some of us are just three generations removed from slavery. If it were not for Harriet (Moses) Tubman, there would be no freedom for those slavesthat sought to be free.

Harriet (Moses) Tubman stated, "I had crossed de line of which I had so long been dreaming. I was free; but dere was no one to welcome me to de land of freedom, I was a stranger in a strange land, and my home after all was down in de old cabin quarter, wid de ole folks, and my brudders and sisters. But to dis solemn resolution I came; I was free, and they should be free also; I would make a home for dem in de North, and de Lord helping me, I would bring dem all dere"

I love Harriet (Moses), Tubman! And I want you to love her too, can't wait to get my hands on those twenty dollar bills with her beautiful face on them, white America, don't try to change shit at the last moment.

In Blackness, there is Color

Written by Glen D. Brady

BLACK IS THE absence of color, the absence of reflected light, the colors that are absorbed; you do not see because black reflects no colors of light to see.

Red, orange, yellow, green, blue, indigo, and violet, are colors that are reflected by white light, that is visible to see.

Like the rainbow across the sky, when the raindrop is lit, by the white light of the sun, you can see a spectrum of colors in the sky.

But that doesn't mean, that the color we bear (black), that these rainbow colors are not there, it's just that black reflects no colors of light, to the naked eyes.

Black is just as beautiful, as the rainbow across the sky, with all the colors, absorb inside.

Don't judge black (me) by what your eyes can't see (stereotypes), know that the same white light of the sun, reflect those same beautiful colors; red, orange, yellow, green, blue, indigo, and violet, in me.

Your eyes might be blue, mine is brown, is not white the color of our teeth, if we both cut our wrist, will we not bleed the same color red, does not the hair follicles on our head, fashion various colors of hair; yellow, black, brown and red.

Black is beautiful, and it is the absence of color, the absence of reflected light,, for the colors that are absorbed, you do not see because black reflects no colors of light to see.

White America you refuse to see me, my colorful heart, my sensitivity, my capabilities and my integrity. You judge me according to the color of my skin (black), and that scares me. Both blacks and whites are wonderfully and fearfully made. We are both beautiful rainbows across the sky when the light of the knowledge of God (the creator) opens, all our eyes to see, all of His beautiful colors, He made the one man (Adam) be.

"I have a dream that my four little children will one day live in a nation where they will not be judged by the color of their skin but by the content of their character."

-Dr. Martin Luther King Jr

To understand the profound meaning of the word, "black," do not seek out its meaning in the Webster dictionary; but in your heart, your goals in life, your dreams and ambition, and then you will realize that; "Black is Beautiful." Stay black, free and proud, for you are are a person of color for the world to see.

-Glen D. Brady

BLACK ON BLACK CRIME

Written by: Glen D. Brady

BLACK ON BLACK crime; sounds like a rhyme, a lyric in a rap song, add some additives like; niggas and bitches, gangsters and hoes. Talk about the hustle, doing whatever it takes to get paid, no moral ode. Talk about money, sex, the selling and the consuming of drugs to trick out the mind (invincibility). Add some fantasizing lyrics about a gangster paradise, murderous row (homeboys). Brag about wearing gold grills and ice out of diamond chains, driving Bugatti Chiron and custom chevrolays. Add in some 808 drum bass beats, some Uzi sounds, 32 rounds (dakka, dakka) with some murderous rhyme, penetrating a reckless killer mind, who do not care about blazing his black brothers or sisters, if they interfere with his grind or the innocent ones on the sideline. Now you got yourself a rap song, black on black crime.

Black on Black crime musically; is engineered by the illuminating Eye (Illuminati) in rap songs; the murderous seduction of the young black mind. Young people are being hypnotized through lyrics and images in rap songs, the seducing 808 drum beats and the cadence of those melodrama rhymes, telling you to destroy your life physically and morally, through immoral rhymes. Rap songs are engineered, organize noise, to extinct the black family; there is no happy ending here, either the grave or a prison cell. I want you to think about this mothers and fathers. Our little black babies at the age of four and five years old, can remember a entire rap song, with its glaring beats, and by the time they get to the 8th grade or 9th grade, most are ready to drop out of school and run the streets. Rap songs impregnate our babies with immoral rhymes, and it grows, maturing in their mind, until it becomes an excessive behavior deliberately engineered to shatter their young black mind.

Rap music is not the only thing that is encouraging Black on black crime. The black family plays a sufficient role also, when it neglect to instruct, discipline,, teach, correct, pray, disciple and encourage their children to discipline their mind, against these immoral, murderous rhymes, engineered to promote black on black crimes, through today's rap music (rhymes).

I am not saying that all rap music is bad and engineered to destroy, the young impressable black mind. Whatever happened to the Sugar Hill sound, the Boogie Down and the Bambaataa sound from back in the day? The block parties in the 80's, even the big momma (your mother, mother; age 60 or older) sitting on her stoop, would tap her feet, to the beat of the positive sound, blasting in the streets. Now a day, black people cannot come together; to enjoy the simple pleasure of unity, without somebody acting like a murderous clown, Hyped up off some murderous soundtrack (rap beat) that he or she has dubbed to be, the anthem for their lifestyle.

Please give some thought to Chuck D quote:

"The powers that be are trying to meld, shape and corral the culture of hip-hop, into another speaking voice for the government."

-Chuck D.

My thought is this; an instrument of destruction (genocide) through rap lyrics, the government is the Ku Klux Klan behind those white sheets (music lables).

NIGGAS WON'T READ OR WRITE

Written by: Glen D, Brady

HELLO, MY NAME is Joe, they say master Brown name me Joe, because his foot was sore, on the day he came down to the slave quarter to see me after I was born, so Joe is my name till the good Lord come and take me, on yonder, They say I was thirteen years old, when Master brown put lye on my eyes, burn out my seeing, for I had taught my self to pronounce and read words, from an old book I found in the horses stable in an old trunk I remember the title of that old book, it was called, the Adventures of Miss Daisy Farnworth and her Dancing Lilies. Those simple words had my interest, words that I would here Master Brown use like; boy, come, you, walk, and run. Hearing these words, and seeing the letters to form them, somehow made me feel alive, it's was like the good Lord open my head, and did something to me. I would cough out a sounds as if someone was teaching me to read, I guess the good Lord figured that niggas need to learn how to read and write too. Mammy was so afraid, for me when I told her, I was reading and writing somewhat, that I learned on my own. Mammy told me about a slave, who got hung for reading when she was a little girl on another plantation. That they hung him on a big tree down in the slave quarters, with a sign around his neck, that said: "NIGGERS DON'T READ."

And all the slave heard about it, that how's Mammy knew what the sigh had said. Mammy begged me to get rid of that old book, she said if the good Lord wants niggers to read, he will tell Master Brown, and Master Brown will tell us what to do. Not often would I disobey my mammy she was good to me, and my sisters and brothers. I think not to tell my little sisters, and brothers, that I can read and write somewhat, for Master might think that they can too, and make an example out of us all, so I hid that old book out in the woods, under a tree. The day when another slave saw me reading, that old book in the woods, and went back, and told Master Brown. That is the day that I knew I had done something right. Though it might cause me my life, for some reason, I wasn't afraid anymore, and IT was like; the good Lord himself was with when the overseers came to fetch me, to take me to Master Brown.

Master Brown was a big man, and he wore a dingy white suite, he had sandy brownish hair and a patchy beard. He always kept a char of chewing tobacco in front pocket of his suit coat, and on that day he had a look on his face, that said; "NIGGERS DON'T READ." Mammy begs Master Brown not to kill me, that I'm just a boy, who don't know, no better. Mammy worked in the big house for years cooking for Master Brown, since I was a baby. Master Brown knew that mammy would not do anything to go against his will, like letting me read. Master Brown said; who taught you to read boy, point him out, but there was not anyone to point out, I learned with myself, with the good Lord's help. Therefore, I stood there with my head down, and my eyes lowered toward the ground, mammy taught us to, never look a white man or a white woman in the eyes, for this is the law of the land for niggas. The word got around that a nigga was caught reading on Master Brown's plantation, the word spread like wildfire. When the older slaves found out that it was me, they said; that boy ain't nothing but trouble for us, a dreamer, and if the good Lord wants niggas to read, he will tell Master Brown, and Master Brown will tell us, what to do. Back then black folks didn't know the time of day, the moth or the year unless they overheard it from the slave master or overseer talking. We knew the time by the rising, and the setting down of the sun, we knew seasons by what we planted and harvest for Master Brown in his fields. Our whole slavery life was based on, what Master Brown told us to be true. At time Master Brown would say;" God made the white man, to rule over the black man, the black man need only to know, what he heeds to do, on the white man plantation. The Black man is no different, then an animal; you care for him, feed him and put him to work".

As I was standing there with my head hung down, and my eyes lowered toward the ground. I felt an urge to say something, I felt alive for the second time in my life, and all of a sudden, I was knockdown to my knees. I heard mammy hollering do not kill him Master Brown; please do not kill my baby. Mammy knew that Master Brown had to kill me, or make an example out of me, for disobeying his rule (no reading), for all the other slaves were there; watching to see what Master Brown was going to do, to me.

The next thing I knew, the overseer had grabbed me and tied me to an old willow tree, the very tree that I love sitting under, in the cool of the day, in the slave quarters when I was a little boy. Then I heard Master Brown tell the overseer to hold my head real tight; I was still feeling a little dazed from being knocked down to my knees, on the ground. I saw Master Brown coming toward me with a bucket, with a stick in it, and I knew that I had seen that bucket before, but I couldn't remember were. Are you wondering why I am telling you all of this, well this is the day; that the good Lord Freed me, from Master Brown plantation. I lost my sight that day; Master brown put lye on my eyes and blinded me for good.

My crying and hollering could have been heard in four countries, they told me that my mammy fainted, and Master Brown told some of the older slaves, to untie me, and take my mammy and me back to tour cabin. Master brown took away my sight, but the good Lord did something better for me, He freed me from slavery in my heard and mind, I am no longer a slave, I am a free man because I learned to read.

I lost my sight, for the cost of freedom, to journey through time, through an old book I found, in an old trunk in the hoses stable, that I was forbidden to read or even to look at, as a slave. Mater Woodrow Brown stilled owns me, but he did not own my mind, some blacks say; he was a good man, I beg the difference. If any young black boys or young black girls are reading or hearing my story, I have been dreaming of they when opportunities are given to black folks to learn how to read and write through reading and writing.

For me, thirty years done passed, and I continue to feel alive, in my heart and mind. Nowadays my hands and ears do my seeing, for me as I work the plantation. As a young man I stagger through Master Brown plantation, he gave strict orders that no one should help me and if anyone did, they will suffer under the lashes of his whip, so I had to make myself useful, through my hands and hearing to be a useful slave for Master Brown.

Somehow, life has been good to me, and the good Lord has always been there for me. My wife and I are raising five children, three of them know how to read and write. Master Brown took my eyes a long time ago, for learning to read and write somewhat, but he could stop the hope that I gave my children to learn to read and write, I told them, like I'm telling you, the only thing that can stop you from reading and writing is you.

Do not be a nigga,, for a nigga is scared to learn, for a nigga will not learn to read or write. Be a prould black man, be a proud black woman, and free your mind from your trouble and learn to read and write, and see the literary world become a place of freedom for you, in your heart and mind, for your accomplishments in this world.

Mr. Young black, and Ms. Young black girl, the cost of reading and writing, has been for, in the loss of; limbs, and life for you to have the opportunities to read and write, a free education. Joe, the slave, would be proud of you all, that his contribution, the loss of his sight, for reading a book which was, forbidden for a slave to do, was not in vain.

Fill in the Blanks with Right Answers

1. Why do McDonalds always run out of happy meals boxes, on the first of the moth _____?
2. Why is the weed man up at 5am, on the first of the month _____?
3. Why do the India liquor store clerk, sound like he speaking clearly on the first day of the month ___?
4. Why do grandmas' be fussing on the first of the month, when her grown ass daughter(s), and those bad ass kids, get that check on the first of the month_____?
5. Why do people sneak and move out of their apartment, the night before the first of the month____?
6. Why do your dog sit near the dinner table, on the first of the moth_____?
7. Why is driving traffic, the heaviest on the first of the month _____?
8. Why do people look happier, and speak to you on the first of the month_____?
9. Why do crack heads be speed walking down the street, with their hands in their pockets on the first of the month_____?
10. Why do the Arab store clerk, do not watch you, like you are trying to steal something, on the first of the month____?
11. Why do baby mommas' talk plenty of shit, to their baby daddy, on the first of the month ____?
12. Why do little kids have the biggest smile on their faces, on the first of the month ____?
13. Why do a single parent family, become a two parent family on the first of the moth ___>
14. Why do Walmart raise their prices up, on the first of the month_____?
15. Why do baby daddies, get the urge to come over, to their baby mamma house on the first of the month, to see this kid(s)_____?

Math the Answers to the Questions:

A. To see if he can get a little, something
B. Special Treat
C. Momma is not cooking shit, on the first of the month
D. They got some money
E. Checking that benefits card, after midnight
F. Early paper
G. He happy to see you, you got money.
H. Going to get, that first hit
I. Got that first rock, in their pocket
J. You got money
K. To get that government money
L. Everybody wants a ride somewhere
M. Chicken Bones
N. Nobody have gave her any money, for watching those damn kids all month
O. Bring her money back, for watching those damn kids
P. Ain't plan on paying the landlord, for this month rent, moving in with a girlfriend or friend
Q. Somebody got some money to spend
R. Done got four hundred dollar worth of shit on credit and trying to run out on the the dope man, you told him; "I pay you on the first of the the month when I get my check."

If you want to make up some answers of your own, to fill in some of the blanks, go right ahead.

Daddy (Nigga) I do not want any Twenty-five cent bag of potato chips, and some candy

Written by: Glen D. Brady

A LITTLE BLACK boy name Marvin, who likes to be called junior, because his dad name is Marvin also, sits on the stoop outside of the apartment building that he and his mom live in, hanging out playing, and talking with the other little kids in the neighborhood. Junior is six years old, and he loves his dad, but junior dad does not live with him and his mom. Junior only see his dad every once, and a while, sometimes months will go by without junior seeing his dad.

However, when his dad did come by, he would take junior to the nearest corner tore, and buy him a twenty-five cent bag of potato chips, a little huggie fruit juice; by the way, junior favorite juice color was red. Dad would buy junior some candy, and then he would take junior, up on the block, as if it were a picture show hanging out with his homies, Junior was happy, not because of the treats, but because he was with his dad, spending some time with his dad. Junior would say to his dad, "Daddy I love you," no matter how many broken promises, junior dad had made regarding coming by, to spend time with him, junior was always ready to tell his dad, that he loves him.

Now it is ten years later, and Marvin aka "junior" is sixteen years old, he is no longer that little boy, wondering when his dad will come by and see him. Junior has become a teenager, with plenty of anger and rage toward his dad; Big Marvin, that is what his mom calls him, Big Marvin, and Big Marvin has not changed a bit, he is still hitting, and missing visits with his son. Now it's not like Big Marvin lives in a different city, or even in the suburbs, Big Marvin lives three blocks away, down the street with his mother. Now you're probably thinking, well if Big Marvin only stays three blocks away from his son, and junior is sixteen now, he can go visit his dad, at this dad mother's house, he is a young man now.

Yes, that is true, but over the years, the lies have hardened junior's heart toward his dad, Big Marvin.

Junior is not that same little boy, who uses to tell his dad that he loved him. Junior has no love, for his dad right now, sometimes junior would say to his mom; I saw that man, and his mom would say; who your dad, and Junior would say; he's no dad to me. One day junior was sitting outside, on the stoop of his apartment building, that he and his mom have been living in, for the past ten years.

Junior chilling with his headphones on, with his head, hung down slightly, nodding and bounce his head somewhat to the beats in the music track. All of a sudden, Big Marvin walks up on him and Junior looked up and seen him, and said: "Nigga I don't want no twenty-five cent bag of potato chips and candy".

Junior said it so quick and so harshly that Big Marvin, hung his head down in shame, and said; I know that now son, can you see it in your heart, to forgive me, for not being a dad to you, when you need me to be.

Junior looked that him, in a funny kind of way; (like are you serious), and in his heart, he wants to tell his dad off. The only words that came out of little Marvin, aka junior, mouth in his anger was, "Daddy I love you", the same words he uses to tell his dad, when he was a little boy. To all you absentee fathers:

"Daddy (Nigga) I don't want no twenty-five cent bag of potato chips and candy" when you do come around, I want to spend some time with you. "It is easier to build strong children than to repair broken men."

-Frederic Douglass

BARACK HUSSEIN OBAMA, THE SECOND THE 44TH PRESIDENT OF THE UNITED STATES OF AMERICA

Written by: Glen D. Brady

BARACK HUSSEIN OBAMA is the first Black African American to have served as President, and if I had the opportunity to ask him a question, I would probably ask him, how many times did he think, white America called him a nigga? The funniest thing about asking him a question is the way, President Obama responds to a question. He would pause for a few seconds and say; hum good question, and It seems like he is putting that Harvard law degree to work (laugh). Here is what I think President Barack Obama would probably say; well after my first one hundred days in the oval office, I told Michelle that I was going to hire a private secretary to record just that. How many times that I have been called a nigga as the President of the Free World, Michelle just look looked at me with a smirk on her face, and I took that to mean; O' buddy here we go. After eight years of serving the American people, as the President of the United States of American. I can truly say that I have been called a nigga approximately 5.3 million times, a bitch ass nigga 4.7 million times, a dog ass nigga 3.5 million times, a punk ass nigga 2.7 million times and a black ass nigga 1.8 million times. And these numbers were recorded just in the legislative body; the Senators and the House of Representatives (Laugh). President Obama always finishes his answer by saying something uplifting like; American citizens, where you are red, white, black, or brown. We can all learn to grow from this point on, that is not about how many times, you have been called a nigga, but knowing that you are not a nigga, is what count in the eyes of this country. Walking in dignity and in pride as a black man, proud to be an American, but even prouder to be a Black American of African descent.

The Obamas are moving out, and the Trumps are moving in the the White House in 1600 Pennsylvania Avenue. A moving transition takes place on the day of the president-elect inauguration day.

In which the incoming president cannot move in until noon, on the day of the inauguration. Nothing can be touched until the Obamas pull out of the White House driveway for the final time as President of the United States of America. I cannot say what President Obama mindset is at this point, as he looks back at the White House through the rear view mirror of his limousine.

President Obama is a black man like me, and probably like other black men with a sense of humor, who have reached, a high pinnacle in white America, a few things come to my mind, as he is holding Michelle's hand while sitting in the back seat of the limousine. I can picture him lean over passionately and gently whisper in her ear, saying; girl, I been knocking those boots, in the White House for eight good years. Those bed sheets are historical and should be placed in the Smithsonian Institution. Michelle, all giggly like a young girl blushing, tapping Barack on his leg, and say; boy you are crazy funny. (Laugh)

The second thing that I can picture is President Barack Obama holding up his index finger while sitting in the backseat of the limousine as it slowly makes its way down the driveway. Telling Michelle; baby I was the (HNIC) Head Nigger In Charge for eight years, they didn't know who they are messing with, I'm Barack Hussein Obama, the Second, I'm a bad man. You know it Michelle, and Michelle is smiling and saying you are a bad man baby, you are a bad man, tells the limo driver he is driving too slowly.(Laugh)

The third thing that I can picture is President Barack Obama being infuriated as he and Michelle are sitting in the backseat of the limousine, discussing how even to the last moment, white America prejudice, with a Black president still pissed him off. Telling Michelle; he should have have painted the White House black like he wanted to do the first year, he was elected. Michelle turned toward him and said; yes, we should have painted it, red, black, and green.

Barack slapping Michelle a high five saying; red: for the blood, Michelle respond, black: for the (black peep's) people, and together they say, green: the abundant natural wealth of Africa. As they laugh wildly at their saying, as their limousine travel down Pennsylvania Avenue.

"Change will not come if we wait for some other person or some other time. We are the ones we've been waiting for: We are the change that we seek."
                                                                    -*Barack Hussein Obama*

No matter how prominent black man or a black woman might become, they still have some blackness with them, to address any issue that they might encounter, with some light humor.
                                                                    -*Glen D. Brady*

CPSIA information can be obtained
at www.ICGtesting.com
Printed in the USA
BVHW061638060522
636307BV00009B/576